A GOLDEN BOOK • NEW YORK

BARBIE and associated trademarks are owned by and used under license from Mattel, Inc.
Copyright © 2003 Mattel, Inc. All Rights Reserved.
Published in the United States by Golden Books, an imprint of Random House Children's Books,
a division of Random House, Inc., New York, and simultaneously in Canada by Random House
of Canada Limited, Toronto. No part of this book may be reproduced or copied in any form
without written permission from the copyright owner. Golden Books, A Golden Book, and
the G colophon are registered trademarks of Random House, Inc.
www.goldenbooks.com
Library of Congress Control Number: 2002113656   ISBN: 0-307-10589-X
PRINTED IN CHINA   10 9 8 7 6 5 4 3 2 1

Barbie™

STARRING
Barbie
#1

A Dream Come True!

By Alison Inches
Illustrated by Karen Wolcott

Cover photography by Tom Wolfson, Susan Kurtz, Tim Geisen, Sawako Iizuka, Scott Meskill, Lisa Collins, and Judy Tsuno

*B*arbie stars in a show by her community theater group, and a famous movie director notices her wonderful performance.

"What a talent!" says the director, Mr. Barrett. "Barbie's perfect for my next film."

After the play, Mr. Barrett introduces himself to Barbie.

"How would you like to audition for my new movie, *The Secret*?"

"Would I ever!" says Barbie as her eyes light up. She has always wanted to be in the movies.

Barbie goes to the movie studio the next day.
She reads lines from *The Secret* for Mr. Barrett.
"The jewels are hidden," says Barbie, reading
from the script. "And you'll never find them."

MAKEUP

Mr. Barrett claps. "Bravo!" he says. "You've got the part of the countess in my new movie. The shoot starts next month."

"Wow!" cries Barbie. "The movies! This is a dream come true!"

On the first day of the shoot, Barbie meets the cast and crew. Mr. Barrett is busy giving instructions to some of the actors on the set.

"Places, everyone!" says Mr. Barrett.
The actors take their positions.
"Action!" he cries.

A production assistant takes Barbie to
Costume Design.
    "Look at all these beautiful clothes!"
says Barbie.
    Then Barbie tries on her countess outfit.

After her costume fitting, Barbie goes to
Hair and Makeup.

When she's all ready, the stylist turns
Barbie toward the mirror.

"Wow!" says Barbie. "I feel like royalty."

On the movie set, Barbie meets the leading lady, Laura O'Neil. Barbie watches Laura get ready for one of the most dramatic scenes in the movie. Laura reads the letter in her hand, and then she starts to cry.

After the scene is over, everyone applauds.

"That was terrific," says Barbie.
"Laura's a great actress."

There is a lot of activity on the set. The gaffer makes sure the lighting is perfect. Then the cinematographer adjusts his camera right before he rolls the film.

"Wow," says Barbie. "A lot of people sure are needed to make a movie happen."

Now it's time to film Barbie's scene.
"Roll 'em!" shouts Mr. Barrett.
"The jewels are hidden," says Barbie.
"And you'll never find them."

Mr. Barrett tells Barbie to act angry and storm out
of the room. After a few takes, the scene is perfect.
Mr. Barrett is pleased with Barbie's performance.
"Great job, Barbie!" he says through his megaphone.

After Mr. Barrett finishes making *The Secret*, he throws a cast party. Everyone has a great time.

When *The Secret* hits movie theaters, the critics love it, and Laura O'Neil is nominated for a Shining Star Award.

THE SECRET

THE TIMES

LAURA NOMINATED FOR SHINING STAR AWARD

The Secret
★★★★★

Mr. Barrett has an extra ticket to the Shining Star Awards, and he sends it to Barbie.

Barbie wears her new satin gown and shawl.

"This is so exciting," Barbie says. The cameras flash as she walks down the red carpet to the awards show.

At the ceremony, the host announces the winner
for best actress. He tears open the envelope.
"And the winner is . . .

. . . Laura O'Neil!"

The orchestra plays music from *The Secret* as Laura walks onto the stage. She holds her golden trophy high.

"Wow," says Barbie. "Laura's wonderful. I've learned so much from her and from all of you."

"You *have* learned a lot, Barbie," says Mr. Barrett.

"And, who knows, maybe you'll star in your
own movie one day soon."

Barbie™

Here are some great Barbie™ storybooks to collect!

STARRING BARBIE™ SERIES

BARBIE™ RULES SERIES

PASSPORT SERIES

HORSESHOE CLUB SERIES

LITTLE GOLDEN BOOKS®